Traditional poem illustrated
by Timothy J. Bradley

Teddy Bear, Teddy Bear,
turn around.

Teddy Bear, Teddy Bear,
touch the ground.

Teddy Bear, Teddy Bear,
tie your shoe.

Teddy Bear, Teddy Bear,
that will do.

Teddy Bear, Teddy Bear,
go upstairs.

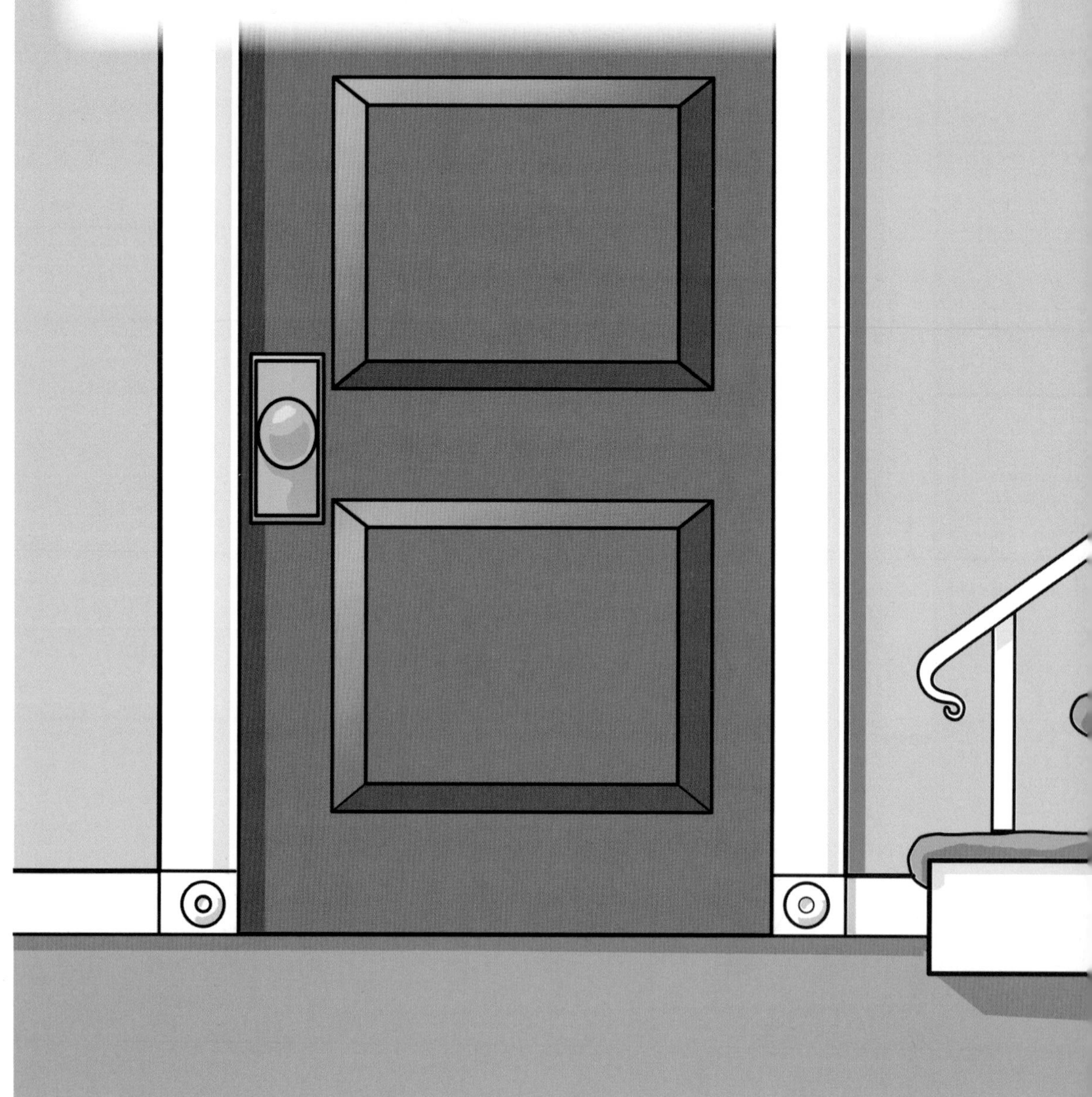

Teddy Bear, Teddy Bear,
say your prayers.

Teddy Bear, Teddy Bear,
turn out the light.

Teddy Bear, Teddy Bear,
say good night.